TECH TEAM

?

Raintree is an imprint of Capstone Global Library Limited, a company incorporated in England and Wales having its registered office at 264 Banbury Road, Oxford, OX2 7DY – Registered company number: 6695582

www.raintree.co.uk
myorders@raintree.co.uk

Printed and bound in China.

ISBN 978 1 474 72053 3 (paperback)
20 19 18 17 16
10 9 8 7 6 5 4 3 2 1

British Library Cataloguing in Publication Data
A full catalogue record for this book is available from the British Library.

Cover art and illustrations by Heath McKenzie

TECH TEAM

AND THE DROID OF DOOM

By Melinda Metz

Illustrated by Heath McKenzie

raintree

a Capstone company — publishers for children

1

"Why did the robot go to the cinema and get popcorn and a drink?" Caleb Quinn asked his best friends, Zoe Branson and Jaden Thomson. It was Monday morning, and they were headed to the Hubble Primary School media centre.

"Wait. *You're* telling a joke? Dumb jokes are Jaden's thing," Zoe protested. Jaden loved to tell them so much that Zoe had to give him a limit of three a day. More than that and she was sure her brain would go *squish*.

"There can never be enough dumb jokes," Jaden said. "Go ahead, Caleb. Why did the robot go to the cinema and get popcorn and a drink?"

"So it could blend in with human society and ultimately conquer it." Caleb didn't smile as he gave the punch line.

Jaden burst out laughing. "Nice!"

"Not nice – and not funny," Caleb told him. "I couldn't believe they had the joke in *Synch*. My favourite tech magazine should know that there's nothing funny about a robot with artificial intelligence. Get enough robots together, and they'll take over the world. I don't even know if Tech Team should be making a robotic dog."

Caleb, Jaden and Zoe were all in Tech Team – Hubble Primary School's science club. They'd known each other since Year 1, but it wasn't until they'd started Year 6 and joined Tech Team that the three had become best friends. Once they were in the group, they'd realized they liked all the same stuff – comics, video games, puzzles and anything science fiction.

At the moment, all eleven Tech Team members were working on building a toy robotic dog they'd named SpotBot. Caleb, Jaden and Zoe were working on its programming. It was their job to write simple step-by-step instructions for the robot in a language SpotBot's  computer brain could understand. The goal was to get the robot dog to act as much like a real dog as possible.

"We're just trying to get SpotBot to react to certain situations and actions in a specific way," Zoe reminded Caleb. "Like the program we just finished – someone pets SpotBot, so it wags its tail. It doesn't actually think for itself."

"Exactly. Besides, Mrs Ram wouldn't let us work on anything unsafe," Jaden told him. Mrs Ram, short for Mrs Ramanujan, was the leader of Tech Team as well as the

Year 6 science teacher. She was a big nerd too, just like them. "The SpotBot will..."

Jaden's words trailed off as he opened the door and walked into the media centre. A woman was shouting over by the checkout desk. It was Ms Kinney, the drama teacher. And she was shouting at Mr Leavey!

Mr Leavey was the school librarian. He was almost like a second sponsor for Tech Team. He'd helped Mrs Ram get the back of the media centre turned into a makerspace for the kids. The makerspace was a community area that had all kinds of supplies and equipment so kids could collaborate on ideas, robotics, science and computers.

"You think your Tech Team kids are so special," Ms Kinney continued. "Well, they aren't. It's not fair that they get advantages the other kids don't!"

Jaden, Zoe and Caleb hesitated in the doorway. They exchanged worried looks. What was she talking about?

"Yeah, they get all kinds of cool equipment, like a 3-D printer, but now we don't even get to do a play because

of the budget cuts!" Mike Perez cried from his spot at Ms Kinney's side. Mike was the president of the drama club. "We'd already started building the sets."

"I'm upset about the budget cuts too, but I–" Mr Leavey began.

Ms Kinney gave an irritated snort. "Come on, Mike. Nothing we say will make any difference." She turned and stalked towards the door. Mike followed right behind her. Caleb, Zoe and Jaden moved out of their way.

Mike stopped and glared at them. "Tech Team won't always be so lucky," he threatened.

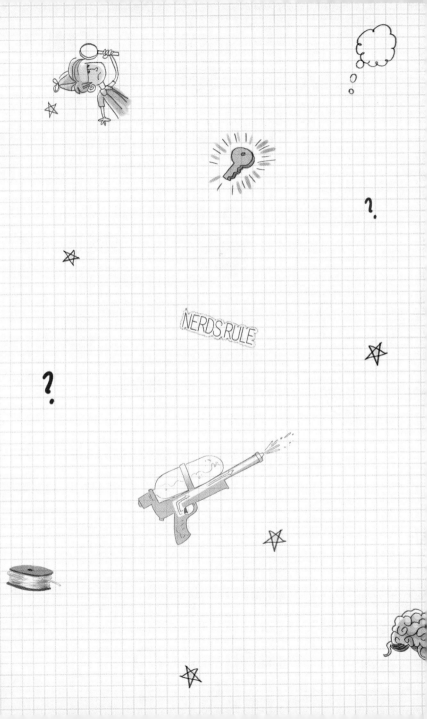

NERDS RULE

2

"What was that all about, Mr Leavey?" Jaden asked as he, Caleb and Zoe walked over to the librarian.

Mr Leavey sighed. "The school just came out with a new budget, and unfortunately the drama club and lots of other school programmes lost money."

"It sounded like they were blaming you – and Tech Team," Zoe said. Her brown eyes were filled with concern.

Mike's words banged around in Caleb's brain. *Tech Team won't always be so lucky.* It didn't sound like Mike was just *blaming* Tech Team. It sounded like he was plotting revenge!

"Tech Team is one of the few programmes that didn't have its budget cut," Mr Leavey explained. "Ms Kinney and her drama club pupils think that's unfair because the makerspace already has a lot of expensive equipment. I tried to explain that the money didn't come from the school – Mrs Ram and I got grant money for the things like your 3-D printer – but they wouldn't listen."

Mr Leavey sighed again. Most of his shirt had come untucked, and he'd missed one belt loop. The librarian kept the whole media centre in perfect order, but he didn't always keep himself so neat.

"But you three don't need to worry about the budget. What happened to the drama club has nothing to do with Tech Team," Mr Leavey said. Then for the first time since the kids had come into the media centre, he smiled. "Get on back to the meeting. Mrs Ram has a surprise for you."

"Oooh! A surprise!" Zoe exclaimed. She practically skipped as she led the way to the makerspace.

"Great, you're here! That's everybody!" Mrs Ram called when she saw Caleb, Jaden and Zoe. "I could hardly wait another second to show you all the surprise!" She hurried over to something draped with a sheet. It was just over a metre tall and not very wide.

Caleb's breath caught in his throat as Mrs Ram whipped the sheet away. A robot stood there, motionless. Its metal body gleamed in the fluorescent light.

"He's so cute!" Zoe gushed. The robot had enormous eyes, no nose and a smiling mouth.

"I think he's cute too," Mrs Ram agreed, patting the robot's head lightly. The back and sides of his head were made of see-through plastic,

revealing circuits and wires. "Dr Wiley, a friend of mine who's a professor at the university, led the team that made him. He wanted the robot to spend some time with kids your age, so I immediately volunteered Tech Team."

"How amazing is The Ram?" Sonja, one of the other Tech Team members, asked the group. Everybody clapped and cheered.

"So are you ready to meet him?" Mrs Ram asked. "All I have to do to turn him on is say his name."

"Yes!" all of Tech Team yelled. All except Caleb. He backed up a step. Although he was curious and wanted to see the bot in action, he needed the option of a fast getaway.

Mrs Ram turned towards the robot. "Dude, welcome to Hubble Primary School."

As soon as she said "Dude", the robot's big eyes opened and moved from side to side, scanning the room. Its ears tilted forward. At least Jaden thought the paddle-shaped objects sticking out from each side of the robot's head were ears. They both glowed faintly with purple LED lights.

Dude blinked once. His eyelids made a soft clicking sound. "It is good to see you again, Mrs Ram," he said.

Caleb gulped and took another step backwards. The robot turned its head in Caleb's direction, as if reacting to the motion. "Hello, Caleb."

The robot said his name! It recognized him! It knew too much! Far too much!

"It's going to take over the world!" Caleb screamed. He whirled around and raced towards the door, yelling a last warning over his shoulder: "It's going to make us all its slaves!"

3

Zoe sped around the corner, shoes squealing on the linoleum floor of the corridor. There he was! Caleb had almost reached the main doors leading out of the school.

"Face-recognition software!" Zoe yelled when she thought he was close enough to hear her. She was sure the robot recognizing Caleb was what had sent her friend into The Zone. That's what she and Jaden called it when Caleb got so nervous he almost couldn't function.

Caleb stopped and turned around. "What?" he asked.

Zoe put her hands on her knees and sucked in a deep breath. "Right after you bolted, Mrs Ram explained that Dr Wiley showed Dude pictures of everybody in Tech Team," she told him. "That's how he knew your name." As soon as Mrs Ram had given the explanation, Zoe had taken off after Caleb.

"You all right?" Jaden asked Caleb as he caught up with them. "Did Zoe explain everything?"

Jaden had told Zoe to go ahead without him so that she could reach Caleb as quickly as possible. Jaden moved a bit more slowly than his friends because of his CP, cerebral palsy. CP affected people in different ways. With Jaden, it made one arm and one leg weaker and stiffer. He had to wear leg braces to help him walk. Sometimes he used a wheelchair if he was going over rough ground.

"Yeah. And yeah," Caleb answered.

"So you ready to get back in there?" Jaden asked.

Caleb nodded, and they all started walking back towards the media centre. He hesitated for a second when they reached the makerspace, then led the way over to the worktable he and his friends shared. The three kids quietly sat back down.

"Who else has a question?" Mrs Ram asked.

Benjamin and Samuel – identical twins nicknamed Thing One and Thing Two after the characters in a Dr Seuss book – raised their hands at exactly the same time. The robot turned its head towards them.

Caleb shivered. *It's just programmed to react that way to motion*, he told himself. He looked over at Benjamin and Samuel too. It was better than looking at the bot.

"You're up, Things," Mrs Ram said.

"What does your friend want–" Thing One began.

"–the robot to learn from us?" Thing Two concluded.

"Dude's job is going to be tutoring kids around your age. He's what's called a social robot. That means a bot that's designed to interact with humans," Mrs Ram explained. As soon as she began to speak, Dude turned his head to look at her.

"Observing and interacting with you will help Dude learn the best way to make the kids he works with feel comfortable," Mrs Ram continued, pacing back and forth. She always did that when she got excited about something, and she was always excited when she talked about science. "He'll see your facial expressions and the gestures you use, and then he'll start to imitate them in the right situations."

"Hold on!" Caleb cried.

Zoe got ready to grab him. She didn't want to have to go running after him again. But Caleb stayed in his seat.

"You're saying it doesn't have to be programmed? It can learn just by watching us?" Caleb continued, running his fingers through his dark hair.

Mrs Ram nodded, and the little superhero shields on her necklace jangled. "A social robot like Dude needs to be able to learn the way a person would. Part of how we learn to behave is by seeing how other people respond to us – not just by what they say, but by the expressions on their faces and their body language."

"What's body language?" Zoe asked.

"It's how the way we hold our bodies shows our emotions," Mrs Ram explained. "You're studying dog behaviour as part of your work on SpotBot. Think about how much a dog's body tells you about how it's feeling."

"Like ears back, tucked tail and hair on the neck standing up," Jaden said. "That means a dog is afraid, but that it might also attack."

human fear

dog fear

"Exactly!" Mrs Ram exclaimed. "And people shrug to show we don't know something. We might ball up our fists if we're angry or cross our arms if we're feeling anxious or afraid."

Caleb realized he had his arms crossed tightly across his chest. He forced himself to put them down by his sides.

"We can help Dude learn to be the best tutor possible if we all just treat him the way you'd treat any new member of Tech Team," Mrs Ram told them.

Zoe stood up. If a new kid joined Tech Team, she'd go over and say hi. Caleb whispered a frantic "Stop!" as she started towards Dude, but she ignored him.

"Hi, Dude. I'm Zoe," she said when she reached the robot. "But you already know that, don't you?"

"Yes. It is good to meet you, Zoe," Dude said. The corners of his mouth rose in a smile.

Zoe turned to Mrs Ram. "His voice sounds almost real. I mean, almost like a person's, but not quite." She winced, then looked over at Dude. "I'm sorry. That was rude. I shouldn't talk about you as if you're not there."

"That is okay, Zoe," Dude replied.

"Human speech is hard to copy because it's so complex," Mrs Ram explained. "There are about forty basic sounds in the English language. But they can be combined in an almost infinite number of ways."

"So how do they make voices for robots like Dude?" Zoe asked her teacher.

"First, technicians start by recording hours of people speaking all kinds of sentences," Mrs Ram said. "Then the sentences are chopped up into sounds that the robot can combine to make any word. This process works well enough for us to understand what Dude is saying, but not quite well enough for him to sound absolutely human."

"It's a good thing they can't sound completely like us," Caleb muttered. "We need to be able to work out who's real and who isn't."

One of Dude's ear paddles – the one closest to Caleb – flicked. Had it heard what he said? Caleb hoped not. He didn't want a robot for an enemy!

"Another problem is that our voices change depending on how we're feeling," Mrs Ram continued. "Think about it. When you're mad, you might talk louder. When you're upset, your voice might get higher. When you're nervous, you might talk faster. A sophisticated robot can almost duplicate these differences in volume, pitch and speed. But it's hard for a robot to decide *when* to use an angry voice or an upset voice. Working out which emotion is appropriate for a specific situation is tricky for them."

"Tricky," Dude repeated.

Zoe still stood in front of the robot. She thought for a second about what she'd do next if she was talking to a new Tech Team member. "Want to work with me and my friends on our project?" she offered.

Dude nodded.

"Great! Come on!" Zoe led the way over to the worktable she shared with Jaden and … *Caleb*! She'd been so focused on how she should be treating Dude that she'd forgotten how she should be treating Caleb. Would bringing Dude over freak him out?

Too late to worry about it now. She and Dude had already reached the table.

"You can sit here," Zoe told him, pulling out the chair next to hers. Dude sat down, his motions smoother than Zoe thought they'd be. "You know Jaden and Caleb," she said.

Dude smiled again. "Hello."

Jaden grinned. "Hi, Dude!"

"We need to get to work," said Caleb, ignoring the bot. He started playing a dog-training video on their computer monitor. They'd been watching all kinds of clips on dog behaviour for ideas on how to program SpotBot. The trainer on the screen started talking about how some dogs became destructive if they were left alone too long.

Zoe noticed Dude's ear paddles lower a little and his mouth curve down. Was he feeling bad that Caleb hadn't bothered to say even one word to him?

Before Zoe could find out, Sonja came up to the table. "Dude, come and sit with me," she said. "My group's trying to work out how to give SpotBot better balance. He tips over too easily at the moment."

"Thanks, Sonja," the robot replied. "But I am going to work with Zoe and her friends."

Sonja scowled at Zoe. "I'm one of Zoe's friends too."

Dude turned his head towards Zoe. "Can you explain what your project is?" he asked.

"We're all working on the same project!" Sonja cried. "Dude's supposed to be for all of us, and you're completely hogging him, Zoe!" She stomped away before Zoe could answer.

Zoe stared after her. She'd sounded so mad. And all Zoe had been trying to do was make Dude feel welcome!

4

"The development of full artificial intelligence could spell the end of the human race!" Caleb told Zoe and Jaden as they walked into school the next morning. "And that's not me saying it. That's Stephen Hawking, the most famous physicist and cosmologist in the entire world! And Stuart Russell, a big artificial intelligence researcher, says AI could be as dangerous as nuclear weapons! And–"

Zoe and Jaden exchanged a look. It was clear Caleb needed to calm down. "Let's go to the media centre," Jaden suggested. "I bet we can also find quotes from scientists who think AI will improve the world."

But they didn't have time to search for quotes. As soon as the friends stepped inside the media centre, Caleb spotted Mrs Ram in the makerspace. "Mrs Ram's here!" he said. "I want to tell her what Stephen Hawking said." He rushed over. Zoe and Jaden were right behind him.

"What happened in here?" Zoe exclaimed. The makerspace was a mess! Her eyes flicked from knocked-over chairs to wires scattered over the floor, to – Dude!

The bot sat motionless on Mrs Ram's desk, eyes closed. Mrs Ram was gently examining one of his fingers. It was broken!

Zoe hurried over. "Is Dude going to be okay?" she asked Mrs Ram.

As soon as he heard his name, the robot opened his eyes and smiled. "What is wrong, Zoe? You look upset."

"Someone br…" Zoe let her words trail off. How was she supposed to tell Dude someone had broken his finger?

"It looks like one of your fingers has been damaged,"
Mrs Ram told Dude. "You go back to sleep, and I'll fix you
up." Dude immediately powered down again.

"Who would've done this?" Jaden asked. He picked up a
broken circuit board. Most of what had been damaged had
come from the worktable he shared with Zoe and Caleb.

"I know who," Caleb said. "The only person – I mean *thing* – that was in here last night." He pointed at Dude. "It!"

"You think he broke his own finger?" Zoe demanded.

"Maybe it happened when the droid was smashing up our stuff," Caleb answered.

"Not possible," Mrs Ram said as she plugged in a soldering iron and began working on Dude's finger. "I powered him down before I left last night. He didn't come back on until Zoe said his name."

"Are you sure you didn't forget to shut it down?" Caleb asked Mrs Ram. "Or maybe it could've been pretending it was off." His friends and his teacher thought the robot was safe. They acted as if it was just a nice, normal person. It was up to Caleb to protect them if they were wrong.

"I'm sure I gave him the sleep command," Mrs Ram said. "But even if I had forgotten, he's programmed to power down after an hour with no interaction."

"Wouldn't someone breaking his finger power him up?" Jaden asked.

Mrs Ram shook her head. "At the moment he only responds to the voice command. You have to say his name."

"See," Zoe told Caleb, crossing her arms. "He was definitely asleep when it happened, so he couldn't have done it."

"We have a mystery," Jaden announced. "Who smashed up our makerspace and broke our robot's finger?"

* * *

The neurons in Jaden's brain felt like they were firing twice as fast as usual. That always happened when there was a mystery to solve. As soon as he, Zoe and Caleb were settled at their usual table at lunch, Jaden launched into a discussion of the case.

"The crime couldn't have happened when the media centre was open," he said. "Mr Leavey would've heard."

"That's why I'm saying the robot did it during the night!" Caleb insisted as he unwrapped his tuna sandwich. "Maybe it even broke its own finger so no one would suspect it. It's not like it feels pain."

"Mrs Ram said Dude was powered down," Zoe reminded him. Jaden nodded.

"The robot can learn without being programmed," Caleb told them. "That's why it's here – to learn by observing and interacting with us. Maybe it learned to ignore the sleep command. And like I keep saying, it was all alone in the makerspace after the media centre was closed."

"Maybe not," Jaden said. "Everybody in Tech Team has a key to the media centre. Someone could've been there this morning."

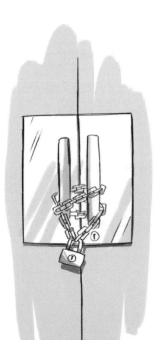

After solving a mystery involving their 3-D printer, the Tech Team had used the printer to make the keys. They'd made a lock and chain too. Now when he left for the night, Mr Leavey looped the chain through the double doors of the media centre and snapped on the lock.

The Tech Team kids were allowed to use their keys to get into the media centre when it was closed so that they could use the makerspace. They could only go in an hour before school and three hours after, though. Once the school building was locked, there was no way to get in.

"Why would anyone in Tech Team break makerspace equipment?" Caleb demanded. "What's the motive?"

Zoe shrugged. Caleb had a point. Then she remembered something important. "Kids in Tech Team aren't the only ones with keys. We made keys for Mr Leavey to give to other club sponsors, remember?"

"Right!" agreed Jaden. "So the first thing we have to do is find out who else has a key. We'll have to get the names from Mr Leavey. Once we know who–"

BANG! The sound of a metallic crash interrupted him. The sound came again as Mike Perez leaped up onto a table, hitting a big pot with a metal spoon. He began to rap to the beat. "What's next? That's what I want to know. Now that Tech Team have stolen our show."

Two more drama kids jumped up from their seats and started dancing down the aisle, clapping along to the beat of Mike's drumming. "What's next? That's what we want to know. Should the football team give up their dreams?"

Three more drama kids sprang to their feet. They circled the table where Zoe, Jaden and Caleb sat. "What's next?" they cried. "That's what we want to know. Tech Team gets a robot, but what have we got? Tech Team gets a robot, but what have you got?"

Everyone in drama club was standing now. "Nothing!" they shouted. "We've got nothing!"

The girl closest to Zoe – Madison Gilman, the drama club vice president – flung out her arms, knocking Zoe's tray into her lap. In the silence that followed the flash mob's performance, someone began to applaud.

It was Ms Kinney. She stood in the back of the lunchroom, clapping so hard that Zoe was surprised her palms didn't burst into flames.

Mike and the drama kids gave deep bows. Slowly, other kids began clapping too, until everyone in the canteen was clapping.

Everyone except the Tech Team.

5

"Where's Caleb?" Zoe asked later that afternoon. "I thought we decided to meet at your locker straight after school." She rubbed the ketchup stain on her favourite skirt. "Thanks a lot, Madison," she muttered.

Jaden shrugged. "Caleb isn't exactly predictable."

Zoe pulled her phone out of her backpack and did a time check. "He's ten minutes late. How much longer should we wait?" They were already supposed to be at the media centre to get the list of people with keys from Mr Leavey. Then they were going to do some extra work on SpotBot.

"There he is." Jaden had spotted Caleb turning the corner and starting down the corridor – slowly.

Zoe noticed Caleb's shoulders were slumped, and his eyes were on the floor as he walked. "Observing his body language, I'd say Caleb isn't feeling happy," she said softly.

"I … um, I just wanted to tell you I … have something to do," Caleb mumbled when he reached them. "You go on without me. I'll meet you at the makerspace when I … when I'm finished."

"Finished with what?" Zoe asked. "You want us to help with … whatever it is?" She'd been irritated that he'd kept her and Jaden waiting, but now she was worried.

"No, I'll just see you down there." With that, Caleb turned and headed off, walking faster.

Jaden stared after him. There was definitely something going on. "You think we should follow him?" he asked.

Zoe considered the question for a moment, then shook her head. "I don't think he feels like talking, at least not at the moment."

"Let's go and talk to Mr Leavey then," Jaden said.

"Yeah, we should get that list of names," Zoe agreed. "I'm curious if Ms Kinney has a key. She's a club sponsor, and we know that she thinks it's unfair that Tech Team didn't have any budget cuts."

"Her, Mike and everyone else in drama club," Jaden added. "That rap they did at lunch showed how mad they are. They definitely have a motive for wrecking our stuff."

They turned down the corridor leading to the makerspace. Mr Figgis, the school caretaker, was mopping the floor and softly singing "Hey Jude". It was an old Beatles song Jaden's dad liked.

"I've never heard you sing before, Mr Figgis," Zoe said as they walked past him. "Sounds good!"

"Oh, thanks. I sing 'Hey Jude' whenever I get nervous," he admitted. "It calms me down."

"You're nervous now?" Jaden asked.

"I don't like spiders," the caretaker confessed. "And I just saw a big one."

Jaden looked around the floor. "I think you're okay. I don't see anything eight-legged."

"Thanks," Mr Figgis said as Zoe and Jaden continued on.

"I'm not sure we should tell Mr Leavey why we want
the list of people with keys," Zoe said as they came to a stop
outside the media centre. "He might not like us thinking of
teachers as possible suspects."

"Already came up with an excuse," Jaden replied, pushing through the door.

They found Mr Leavey working behind the checkout desk. "Could we get a list of the people you gave media centre keys to?" Jaden asked him. "The plastic on mine is getting a little chipped, and we want to make sure no one needs a replacement."

"Yes, I can print out a list," Mr Leavey answered. "Find me before you leave."

"Thanks," Jaden and Zoe said together.

"Uh-oh. We might be turning into Thing One and Thing Two," Zoe teased as they walked back to the makerspace.

All the other kids were there, even though it wasn't an official Tech Team meeting. They must've wanted to get in some extra time working on SpotBot too.

At a nearby table, Mrs Ram was marking homework. Dude stood behind her, eyes rolling from side to side as if he wanted to see everything at once.

"Hi, Zoe," Dude said as soon as he spotted her. He came straight over. "I wanted to ask how your day was."

"I'll go and find some dog videos for us to watch while you and Zoe talk," Jaden said. He walked towards their worktable.

"How was your–" Dude began.

"First I want to see how your finger is." Zoe took the hand with the injured finger in both of hers. "It looks great," she said. "How is it working?"

Dude waggled his fingers. "Mrs Ram did a good job," he answered. "How was your–"

"I can't believe it. You're hogging Dude again!" Sonja exclaimed as she strode over. "He's not your special pet, Zoe."

"I know that, Sonja. I just got here, and Dude was saying hi," Zoe explained.

"Well, I'm sure he's said it, so now it's my turn." Sonja moved closer, trying to push her way between Zoe and Dude. Zoe let go of Dude's hand.

"I would like to talk to you, Sonja," Dude said. "But I just asked Zoe about her day."

"And of course that's more important than anything." Sonja spun around. "Mrs Ram! Zoe's hogging the robot again. It's not fair! Tell her she's already had her turn."

Mrs Ram stood up. "Sonja, I want Dude to be free to act like any kid in our group," she said when she reached them. "That means he should talk to whomever he wants."

"It's okay. I'll go to my workstation. Jaden and I are going to watch some more dog-behaviour videos anyway," Zoe said, backing up. She could talk to Dude later if it was so important to Sonja to get a turn.

But as she started for her workstation, Dude followed her. "Zoe, I would like to hear about your day," he said.

Sonja huffed angrily and stomped over to the supply cabinets. She started taking out metal-working equipment and slamming it down on the worktop. "If this is how it's going to be," Sonja said loudly, "I don't know if I even want to be in Tech Team."

6

"This clip is about a man who spent a year living near a pack of wolves to study their behaviour," Jaden said. They'd been watching dog-behaviour videos for about an hour. "Dogs are related to wolves. We might learn something."

"Okay, then!" Zoe said.

"Okay, then!" Dude agreed. He was still sitting at their worktable, and Sonja had been shooting evil looks at him – and Zoe – every few minutes.

Jaden pressed play, and a man with a scraggly beard started talking about how he'd urinated in a circle around his tent. By marking his area the same way the wolves marked theirs, they would understand the campsite was his territory.

"I'm sorry," Zoe burst out. "I can't focus. I keep thinking about Caleb. He said he was going to come late. He didn't say he wasn't going to show up at all."

"I know," Jaden said. "I've been making notes for him. He's missed some good info, such as how some dogs chew on themselves when they're anxious or are left alone too much. We might want to use some of that behaviour for SpotBot."

When dogs get anxious or are left alone too much, they might chew on themselves.

Pet cones keep dogs from biting and injuring themselves.

Zoe sighed. "I wasn't thinking about all the dog behaviour info he's missing. I'm just worried about him."

"Me too," Jaden admitted.

"Why are you worried?" Dude asked.

"Because our friend wouldn't tell us why he was going to be late," Zoe explained. "It's almost like he was keeping a secret from us…"

"You do not have to worry. Caleb is here," Dude said.

But instead of heading to their workstation, Caleb walked straight over to Mrs Ram. He put a sheet of paper down on her table, then turned to face the other kids. "This is a petition asking Mrs Ram to return the robot to the people who made it – immediately," he announced. "I've already got twenty signatures, and I just started asking people after school."

Zoe put her hand on top of Dude's as Caleb went on.

"Humans aren't at the top of the food chain because we're the strongest," he said. "It's because we're the cleverest. It's dangerous to create something more intelligent than we are. If you don't want to be part of that, if you don't want the robot here, then come up and sign."

Now Jaden knew why Caleb had been late. He'd been getting signatures on that petition. Maybe he'd been practising what he was going to say too. Usually Caleb would just yell about DOOM crashing down on them, and everyone would laugh. But Jaden could see that his argument had got the Tech Team thinking.

Benjamin suddenly leaped up. "We're signing the–" He paused, waiting for his twin to finish the sentence.

But Samuel didn't say a word. He just frowned at his brother.

Benjamin cleared his throat. "I mean, I'm signing the petition." He walked up to the petition and signed it.

"Who else?" Caleb called out.

Antonio stood up and added his name to the petition. When he returned to his worktable, Dylan, who sat at the table too, shook his head.

No one else came forward, but Zoe saw some kids staring at Dude with worried expressions. Sonja still glared at her and Dude. It was very tense and quiet in the makerspace.

Caleb picked up the sheet of paper and carefully folded it. "Let me know if you change your minds. You should also know that I think Dude has advanced to the point where it doesn't have to follow the command to power down. I think it was the one who smashed up the makerspace last night." He put the paper into his backpack and walked away from Mrs Ram's table.

Jaden thought Caleb might keep walking and never come back. Instead, he took his usual seat at their table.

"I don't have any reason to believe that Dude was behind the vandalism of our space," Mrs Ram said, her voice firm. "I would not have given permission to Dr Wiley to bring Dude here if I thought he was dangerous. I don't plan to send him away early. But if any of you would rather not interact with him, I'll arrange for a separate work area until it's time for Dude to leave."

Benjamin and Antonio stayed in their seats. So did Caleb. "You don't want to work somewhere else?" Zoe asked.

Caleb shook his head. "I'm staying. I'm staying, and I'm watching. I'm making sure no one gets hurt while *it's* here," he said loudly enough for everyone to hear.

"Me–" Benjamin paused and looked at his twin "–too." Antonio nodded.

Dude's paddle ears dropped so low they almost touched his shoulders. His mouth curved down. If he had been able to cry, Zoe was pretty sure he would have.

"You do not like me, do you, Caleb?" he asked.

Caleb didn't answer. Dude rose and walked over to Mrs Ram. "I'd like to go to sleep for a while," he told her.

"Of course," she said. "That's fine."

"You don't have to, Dude!" Zoe exclaimed. "You're part of the group. You live right here in the makerspace. This is your home."

Dude didn't answer. Instead, his big eyes closed, and his body went still as he powered down.

Jaden thought maybe a joke would break the tension at their table – and in the whole room – but he couldn't come up with one. That had never happened!

Zoe spun around. "Caleb, you should go and say you're sorry," she told him. "You've really hurt his feelings!"

But Caleb shook his head again and crossed his arms. "I'm not sorry," he said firmly.

7

After Dude powered himself down, everyone in Tech Team continued to work on SpotBot. But there was none of the usual chatter. Zoe was relieved when it was almost time to go home.

"We should go and see if Mr Leavey has the list we wanted," she told Jaden. She glanced over at Caleb. "In case you're interested, we asked him for the names of everyone who has a key to the media centre. So we can work out who *really* smashed up the makerspace."

"If you want to look at other people, I'll help," Caleb answered. "It will take you less time to find out I'm right."

"You mean *you'll* find out *you're* wrong faster," Zoe replied.

It's like all they care about is being right. That's not how it usually is when we're working on a mystery, Jaden thought as he led the way to Mr Leavey's office. He knocked on the door.

"Come in," the librarian called. He looked from Zoe to Jaden to Caleb. "What's wrong with you three?"

Caleb and Zoe didn't answer. "We're okay," Jaden replied, even though it wasn't really true. "Were you able to get that list together?"

"Yep." Mr Leavey took the list off a stack of papers and held it out to Jaden.

As Jaden moved forward to get it, one of his leg braces brushed against the doorframe. That reminded him – Mr Leavey's office had a separate door that led out into the hall. It was across from the one that led to the rest of the media centre. Could the hall door be the way the perpetrator had got in?

"Do any teachers have keys to your office doors?" Jaden asked as he put the list into his pocket.

Mr Leavey raised his eyebrows. "No. Why?"

"You know me. I'm curious," Jaden said.

Mrs Ram popped her head round the door on the media centre side of the room. "I'm off," she told them. "Everybody's out, and our robot friend is still powered off," she said, careful not to use Dude's name so he wouldn't accidentally turn on.

"I think I'll head out too," Mr Leavey announced. The three kids followed him out of his office, and they all walked out of the media centre together. "See you tomorrow," he said as he threaded the chain through the handles of the double doors.

"Hey, Caleb, can I borrow the petition? Just for tonight?" Jaden asked after they'd left Mr Leavey and Mrs Ram behind. Caleb handed it over.

"You're not going to sign it, are you?" Zoe asked, horrified.

"No, but I want to see who *did* sign it," Jaden replied. "A person who doesn't want Dude around has a motive to hurt him." His brow furrowed. "And we can't forget that hurting Dude is only one possible motive for what happened in the makerspace. The perpetrator could have wanted to hurt Tech Team. Breaking Dude's finger and smashing up Tech Team equipment does that."

"Mike threatened us that day we saw him in the media centre. He said we wouldn't always be so lucky, remember?" Caleb asked. "And he's not the only pupil who is mad that Tech Team didn't get any money taken away."

Zoe thought about it. "Plus there are all the people on the petition who don't want Dude at school – that's a lot of suspects. This is going to be a hard case."

?

NERDS RULE

?

8

"Okay, let me show you what I came up with last night," Jaden said before school on Wednesday morning. "We can use it to start a list of suspects."

He, Zoe and Caleb settled on one of the benches in the school's entrance hall, and Jaden pulled a Venn diagram out of his backpack. In one circle was a list of people who had keys to the media centre. In a second circle was a list of people who had signed the petition. The names of people on both lists were in the area where the circles overlapped.

The three kids studied the diagram for a moment. "Mr Webb, the maths club sponsor, signed the petition and has a key. I know because some kids in the club wanted to make some geometric shapes with the 3-D printer. Did he say anything when he was signing the petition, Caleb?" Jaden asked.

"He said the smarter machines get, the faster they can increase their intelligence," Caleb answered. "Biological brains can't do that. They improve slowly, over hundreds of millions of years of evolution. We can't keep up."

"We don't have to keep up," Zoe argued. "We can team up with robots. They can help us do amazing things."

Caleb snorted. "Why would they want–"

"Can we stay focused on the case?" Jaden begged.

Zoe pulled out a notebook and started a suspect list. She wrote down Mr Webb's name and then asked, "Did Mr Figgis give a reason for signing?"

"Just that robots make him nervous. He doesn't like how they look and sound sort of human, but aren't," Caleb answered.

"Makes sense for him to have a key. He has to be able to clean every–" Jaden stopped in mid-sentence as Mr Figgis came around the corner pushing a mop bucket.

"You kids be careful in the halls," the caretaker told them as he paused to wring out the mop. "There are little oily puddles everywhere this morning. I started mopping as soon as I saw them, but I haven't got them all yet."

"We'll be careful," Zoe promised. She rested her hand on the open page of her notebook so Mr Figgis wouldn't see that she'd just added his name to the suspect list.

Jaden studied the diagram again as the caretaker rolled the mop bucket away. "There are only three other people who have keys and signed the petition," he observed.

"You think Benjamin, Antonio or I would smash up Tech Team equipment?" Caleb demanded.

"No," Jaden said quickly. "I just wanted the diagram to be accurate. We should move on to people with keys who didn't sign the petition. They could still be suspects."

"Ms Kinney," Zoe said. "And Mike and Madison. They could have borrowed or taken her key."

"Why would a drama teacher have a key in the first place?" Caleb asked.

"They used some of our equipment to make props," Jaden replied. "Anyone else for the list?"

"There's the Droid of Doom," Caleb answered.

Jaden shook his head. "I think we should leave Dude off unless we get proof that he can ignore the sleep command."

"What about Sonja?" Zoe asked, her voice quiet.

"I thought we just agreed no one in Tech Team would ruin Tech Team equipment," Caleb protested.

"I know, but she has a temper," Zoe reminded him. Everyone knew that Sonja could yell the loudest out of all the Tech Team members and wasn't afraid to do it. "She was really mad that Dude wasn't paying attention to her . . . maybe mad enough to break his finger. And most of the broken stuff was from our worktable. Sonja was mad at me too. She kept complaining I was *hogging* Dude. Maybe she wanted to get back at me and so she smashed some of our stuff up."

"I guess she goes on the list," Jaden agreed.

Zoe added Sonja's name. It felt bad to have a Tech Team member as a suspect, and being thorough didn't make that any easier.

9

Zoe froze when she and the boys reached the canteen for lunch later that day. "I think I left my jumper in the makerspace last night. It has my ID in the pocket!" she cried. She needed her ID to pay for lunch. "I have to go and get it."

"We'll walk down there with you," Jaden told her.

"Thanks! It'll just take a second," Zoe said.

When they got to the media centre, Zoe dashed to the makerspace. Caleb and Jaden followed behind her. "Oh, no," she whispered when she picked up her jumper. There was a big splotch of oil on it.

Caleb felt his heart lurch. "The robot – it's wrecking stuff again."

"Come on, Caleb. That makes no sense," Jaden said.

"It wants to take over the world," Caleb replied.

Jaden sighed. "By ruining Zoe's jumper? That's nuts."

"Where is he, anyway?" Zoe asked. She looked around the room. "Dude! Where are you?

"I am here," Dude said, powering on when Zoe called his name.

But the kids still couldn't see him. Zoe and Jaden rushed towards the sound of the robot's voice. Caleb followed, but cautiously. They found Dude lying on the floor behind the table that Abby, Goo and Sonja shared. His eyes were blinking rapidly. His ear paddles were flipping back and forth.

"My arms and legs cannot move," Dude announced. "Help me, please."

Zoe couldn't help letting out a little scream. "Now his whole body is broken! He can't get up!"

"Do you think we should try to lift him?" Jaden asked.

Before Zoe or Caleb could answer, they heard the sound of pounding footsteps. A few seconds later, Mr Leavey burst into the makerspace and rushed over. "I heard a scream and…" His words trailed off as he caught sight of Dude. "What happened?" he asked.

All three kids tried to answer at once, their words tumbling over each other. Mr Leavey got enough to understand. "I'll go and get Mrs Ram," he told them, running back out.

Zoe crouched down next to the robot, grabbing his hand. "Don't worry, Dude, we're getting help," she promised him.

* * *

Less than five minutes later, Mrs Ram arrived, followed by Mr Leavey. "Give me a little room," Mrs Ram told the kids. She dropped to her knees next to Dude.

"I cannot move my arms or legs," Dude said. "Help me."

"Okay, your battery is charged or you wouldn't be able to talk," Mrs Ram noted. She ran her hand down one of

Dude's legs, then raised her fingers. Jaden saw there was something slick and oily on them.

Mrs Ram took a cautious sniff of the substance. "I think it might be hydraulic fluid," she said. She carefully removed a panel from the front of Dude's thigh. "Yep, Dude's legs – and I'm sure arms too – are powered by hydraulics. We haven't covered that in our lessons yet. Anyone know what a hydraulic system is?"

"A mechanism operated by the resistance offered or the pressure transmitted when a liquid is forced through a small opening or tube," Dude answered.

"That's an A for you, Dude," Mrs Ram said with a smile. "Why don't you go to sleep while we check you over?" The robot shut his eyes.

"I knew what hydraulics are, but I'm not sure how they work in a robot," Caleb admitted.

"See these tubes?" Mrs Ram asked, running a finger down a green tube in Dude's leg. "They work pretty much like the tube inside a water pistol. When you push on the trigger of a water pistol, you force water through the tube inside, and it squirts out of the nozzle. The pressure you put on the trigger translates into the water coming out of the nozzle at a fast speed."

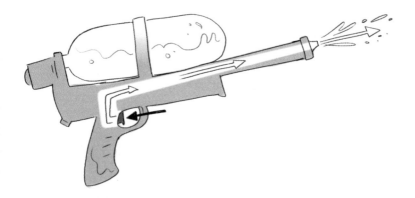

Caleb leaned forward a little, but he didn't want to get too close. Maybe the robot was just pretending its arms and legs couldn't move.

"Hydraulics can also work like a water pistol in reverse," Mrs Ram continued. "Imagine if you could squirt a fast stream of water into the nozzle of a water pistol. The water gets pushed through the tube and pushes the trigger out."

"I think I get it," Zoe replied. "The force of the liquid getting pushed through those tubes makes his joints move, and that makes his legs move."

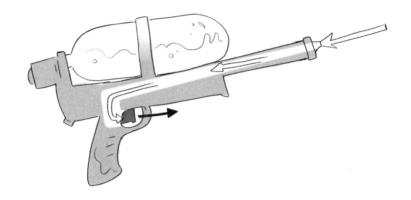

"Exactly! That's what's wrong with his arms and legs," Mrs Ram said. "There's no hydraulic fluid in his tubes, so there's no force to move his joints."

"How did that happen?" Zoe asked.

"I'm not sure. But the tubes have been ripped." Mrs Ram pointed to jagged tears in the tubes. Her forehead wrinkled as she looked down at Dude. "This definitely wasn't an accident. Someone was trying to hurt our robot."

10

"Any clues as to who could have sabotaged him?" Jaden asked when Mrs Ram had finished examining Dude's arms and legs.

Mrs Ram shook her head. "No. And he could have been like this for hours. I didn't have time to stop by the makerspace before lessons started this morning." She stared down at Dude for a moment, then lifted her head up. "You kids need to get to the canteen," she said. "The bell is going to ring soon. I'll give you an update on how he's doing at the Tech Team meeting this afternoon."

Zoe, Jaden and Caleb obediently walked out of the media centre and towards the canteen. "I was right," Caleb said, feeling triumphant.

Jaden gave his friend a puzzled look. "I'm not sure what you mean," he said.

"I said the droid ruined Zoe's jumper, and now you have to admit it. That oily stuff on it has to be hydraulic fluid. Hydraulic fluid from Dude!"

"You think Dude tore open his own tubes so he could spill hydraulic fluid on my jumper?" Zoe demanded. That theory was weird, even for Caleb.

"Not just on your jumper. All over the school!" Caleb exclaimed. "That stuff Mr Figgis was mopping up this morning? I bet it was the hydraulic fluid. The fluid wouldn't have gushed out all at once. It would have dribbled out slowly. So Dude could have made puddles throughout the school – and on your jumper – before it emptied its system and wasn't able to move."

"Why would he do that to himself?" Zoe cried.

Jaden rubbed his face with one hand. "Besides, Mrs

Ram powered Dude off before we left last night. She told Mr Leavey and us that."

"Right!" Zoe agreed. "Somebody – somebody with a key – must have gone into the makerspace after we left, but before the school got locked up for the night. They probably drained Dude's fluid into a jar or bucket or something. Maybe they accidentally sloshed some on my jumper and in the corridors, especially if they were hurrying."

Caleb frowned. "I still say if the bot is smart enough to learn just by spending time with us, then it's smart enough to fake being powered down," he insisted.

"But even if he was on, he'd have been locked in the media centre," Zoe pointed out.

"Unless it went out through Mr Leavey's office!" Caleb shot back. "No lock and chain on those doors. All it'd have to do is turn a couple of door handles, which would've been no problem."

"We're just making guesses about what happened. We need to get some real evidence – fast," Jaden said. "Dude got a broken finger, and our makerspace was smashed up.

Then Dude lost the use of his arms and legs, and Zoe's jumper got ruined. If we don't solve this case fast, what's going to happen next?"

* * *

That afternoon, as soon as everyone in Tech Team was gathered in the makerspace, Mrs Ram explained what had happened to Dude.

"How are you feeling now, Dude?" asked Zoe.

"I am fine, Zoe. Thank you," Dude said, his mouth turning up into a smile. Zoe let out a sigh of relief and smiled back at the robot.

"He wasn't hard to fix," Mrs Ram told them. "I called Dr Wiley during my free period, and he talked me through the repairs." Mrs Ram paused, frowning. "Unfortunately, Dr Wiley and I have decided it isn't safe for Dude to stay with us any longer. A member of Dr Wiley's team will pick him up tomorrow. I'm going to move Dude to the headteacher's office until then. I don't want to risk any more damage to him, and Ms Romero's office is more secure."

Jaden nodded. "Far too many people have keys to the media centre," he said, softly enough that only Zoe and Caleb could hear him.

"It probably won't have any problem getting out of the headteacher's office and doing whatever it wants to do," Caleb whispered back. "But at least it's leaving tomorrow." He took a deep breath. He felt like he hadn't been able to take a good, deep breath for days.

Caleb looks so happy, Zoe thought. She glanced around the room. Antonio looked triumphant. Dylan looked disappointed. Benjamin looked relieved. Samuel looked annoyed.

Jaden thought his friends could really use a joke right now, but he couldn't think of one. That kept happening!

"Come on, Dude," Mrs Ram said. She took him by the arm and led him across the makerspace. "I'll be back in a few minutes," she told the kids.

"Goodbye," Dude called. "Goodbye, Zoe."

"Bye, Dude. I'll miss you!" Zoe called back to the robot.

As everyone started working on SpotBot, Sonja walked over to Zoe. She looked a bit embarrassed.

"Hey, Zoe," she said slowly, "I know you'll miss Dude. I'm sorry he's going. I…" She let out her breath in a huff. "I hate apologizing. But I'm sorry I was mean about how much time you spent with him. You're the friendliest kid in Tech Team, and you were the first one who talked to him. It makes sense that he wanted to spend time with you."

"Thanks, Sonja," Zoe replied. "I'm sure he'd have spent time with everyone if he'd been able to stay." She fiddled with a piece of wire on the table. "At least he'll be safe now."

* * *

Even though Jaden didn't have to worry about Dude getting hurt again, he still wanted to solve the mystery. But he couldn't think what the next step should be. It felt like every time he tried to talk through the case with Zoe and Caleb, all they did was snap at each other.

"Let's spend some time working on SpotBot," Jaden finally said. Maybe he'd get an idea about the mystery while they worked.

"Sounds good to me," Caleb agreed.

"Okay, we want Spot to rip up his pillow if he's left alone for too long," Zoe said. "But from the videos we watched, it seems like there would be other behaviours first. Why don't we start with a loop? Something like if SpotBot hasn't been petted for ten minutes, he whines."

Jaden nodded. "All right." SpotBot had touch sensors on the top of its head and its back, so it would know if it had been petted or not. "How many times should we loop? Four? Five?"

"I think five times works," Caleb answered.

Jaden started dragging and dropping blocks of code onto their computer screen, using the software program they used to do the coding for SpotBot. "I'm putting in that each whine should last twenty seconds," Jaden said as he selected the amount of time from the drop-down menu.

"After that, SpotBot could move from whining to barking," Caleb suggested.

"Then after the barking, we can have him move on to tearing up the pillow," Zoe said.

Caleb smiled. It felt good to be working as a team again. SpotBot didn't make Caleb that nervous. It would only do what it was programmed to do – unlike Dude.

Caleb couldn't help worrying about what Dude would do tonight. He was sure the droid would get out of the headteacher's office. And that would lead to DOOM.

* * *

"Half an hour left! Then it's time to go home," Mrs Ram called out an hour later.

Zoe couldn't believe it was already time to go. She'd got so caught up in programming that she'd lost track of the time.

"How's it going, teams?" Mrs Ram asked.

"We've solved the tipping-over problem," Abby said. She, Sonja and Goo all beamed proudly.

"We're almost finished making changes to the tail so it can curl between the SpotBot's legs, not just wag," Anthony announced.

"And we have code for how SpotBot should behave when it's left alone or ignored," Jaden said. "Do you want to test it out tonight?"

"I'm afraid to leave SpotBot in here," Abby said, wrapping her arms around herself. "What if someone gets in and damages him like they did Dude?"

"We can leave him in my room," Mrs Ram offered.

"I'll grab his pillow," Zoe said. "The program won't work without it."

Sonja picked up the robot dog, and they all went down to Mrs Ram's classroom. Once they had SpotBot settled, they returned to the corriodr. Mrs Ram pulled out her key and locked the door. Caleb immediately tested it. It didn't open.

"Can we meet before school to see if the test run worked?" Jaden asked.

"Absolutely," Mrs Ram said. "I'm as curious as you are. Anybody who has time, meet here half an hour before the first bell."

Sonja planted her hands on her hips, her eyes narrowing. "Nobody better hurt our dog tonight!"

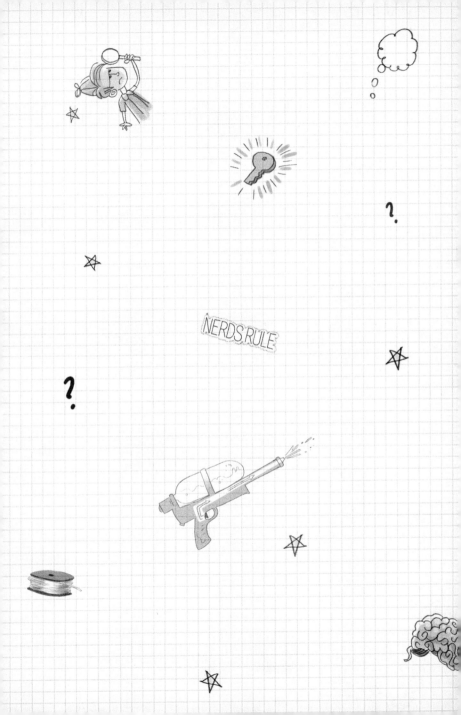

NERDS RULE

11

"I wish I'd had more time to talk to Dude before Mrs Ram took him to the headteacher's office," Zoe said. She and the boys were heading over to Caleb's locker so he could grab a book before they left. "I hardly got to say–"

Zoe was interrupted by a scraping sound. A few moments later, Mike, Madison and some other drama kids dragged what looked like part of a lift made mostly of Plexiglas around the corner.

"I can't believe we won't use this," Madison grumbled. "It was going to be so cool to watch it rise off the stage."

"I know! I still can't believe a water pump could have that much power," Mike said. "But Ms Kinney was right. It was enough to move the lift, even with Charlie and Willy Wonka inside." He let out a moan. "Willy Wonka was the most exciting character I've played. Now no one will ever see my performance."

"Watch out for the drinking fountain," Madison warned. "We're about to hit it."

Mike looked up and squinted – he wasn't wearing his glasses. But Zoe could tell the exact second he spotted her, Jaden and Caleb. His lips tightened into a scowl.

"We wouldn't be throwing this away if Tech Team hadn't taken all the drama club money," Mike said.

"What's next? What's next?" the two other drama kids started to chant, thumping on the side of the lift to the beat of the rap they'd performed in the canteen.

"We didn't get money from–" Jaden began, then stopped. Nothing he said would change how they felt. The friends ignored the drama kids and continued towards Caleb's locker.

"Did you hear what they said about the *water pump?*" Caleb demanded when they'd reached the end of the corridor. "They were using hydraulics to power that lift. They know how hydraulics work."

"Which means they would've known draining Dude's hydraulic fluid would've messed him up!" Jaden exclaimed.

Zoe pulled out the list of suspects she'd made. She put a star by both Mike's and Madison's names. "It sounded like

Ms Kinney came up with the idea for using the pump," she said, adding a star next to Ms Kinney's name too. "That's three suspects who understand hydraulics – and have keys to the media centre. Well, Ms Kinney certainly has a key, and Mike and Madison could have got it from her."

Jaden moved closer to Zoe so he could see the list too. "Sonja is a science nerd. She could've worked out that draining the hydraulic fluid would do a lot of damage. I'm not sure about Mr Figgis or Mr Webb."

"Yeah, but Sonja seemed really sad that Dude had to leave. And she apologized for complaining about how much time Dude spent with me," Zoe said. "I suppose we should leave her on the list and give her a star, just in case, but I don't think she did it."

Zoe added the star, then glanced over at Caleb. He wasn't on the suspect list, but he'd tried to blame Dude for breaking Tech Team equipment and ruining her jumper with hydraulic fluid. Had that been part of a plan to get Dude sent back to his lab?

She nibbled on her lower lip, then darted a look at Jaden. His eyebrows were pulled together the way they always were when he was concentrating hard. She was pretty sure he was thinking the same thing she was.

"You can say it," Caleb told them. "I know about hydraulics too. Plus I started the petition, and I have a key. I'm the perfect suspect. Go ahead. Put me on the list. With a star." He looked from Zoe to Jaden. "But I didn't do it."

12

"Good morning, good morning!" Mrs Ram called as she came around the corner the next day.

Caleb, Jaden, Zoe, Goo, Abby, Sonja and the Things were gathered in front of their teacher's room to see if SpotBot had torn up its pillow the way it was supposed to.

"After you," Mrs Ram told the kids, unlocking the door and holding it wide open.

Zoe let out a cheer when she saw pieces of cotton and scraps of cloth on the floor. "The programming worked!"

"Good little Spot," Abby crooned. "You made a mess just like you were supposed to."

"And he didn't tip over! We did it!" Sonja exclaimed.

"Excellent job, kids," Mrs Ram told them.

"Another robot from the university?" a voice said. "One wasn't enough?"

Zoe looked up and saw Ms Kinney standing in the doorway. She hadn't even heard the drama teacher arrive.

"No, it's–" Mrs Ram began.

Ms Kinney didn't let her finish. "It would be *wonderful* if I had connections at the university the way *you* do. I'd love to have a drama professor come and talk to my pupils, but will they get that opportunity? No! They get nothing, while your Tech Team kids get everything!" Ms Kinney's face had gone from pink to red to maroon in the few moments since she'd arrived.

"Excuse me, please," a woman said. Ms Romero, the headteacher, squeezed past Ms Kinney and into the room.

"You're just who I wanted to see!" Ms Kinney exclaimed. "It is completely unfair that the–"

"We can talk later, Ms Kinney," the headteacher said firmly.

Ms Kinney huffed. "I'll be in my classroom if you manage to find a few minutes for me, Ms Romero." With that, the drama teacher whirled around and stormed off.

The headteacher turned to Mrs Ram and the Tech Team "I'm so sorry to tell you this," she began. "I don't know how it could've happened. I really don't."

She was about to say something very bad. Caleb knew it.

Ms Romero cleared her throat and went on. "Somehow between when I left my office last night and when I arrived this morning, your robot was attacked!"

* * *

Mrs Ram, Zoe, Caleb, Jaden and the other kids hurried out of the room and down to the main office. All the air went out of Zoe's lungs when she saw Dude.

A deep dent had been bashed into the aluminium of the robot's leg, so deep that the wires and tubes underneath were visible in places. Zoe was glad Dude was in sleep mode. She knew he couldn't feel pain, but it would be horrible for him to know someone had attacked him like that.

Jaden nodded to the brass owl paperweight on the floor near Dude. It was about thirty centimetres tall. "That has to be the weapon."

Benjamin looked at his twin. "Someone really wanted to–" He paused briefly. "Destroy him." Samuel didn't reply.

"I just don't understand how it could've happened," Ms Romero said. "I locked the office door myself." She sighed. "I feel terrible. It was such a wonderful opportunity for you all to study the robot. I was hoping it would lead to more collaboration between our school and the university. But that won't happen when we can't be trusted to take care of such valuable equipment."

Zoe hated hearing Dude called "valuable equipment". But at least the headteacher was upset about what had happened. She glanced over at Caleb. He didn't look happy, but he didn't look upset either. He was just staring at Dude with a blank expression on his face.

Zoe's stomach turned over. Could Caleb have done this?

13

"I think Ms Kinney is our top suspect," Jaden said that day at lunch. "We saw how furious she was this morning. And it didn't sound like she knew Dude was going back to the university. Someone who knew Dude was being sent away wouldn't have had a motive to go after him."

Zoe pulled out their list of suspects. "Madison and Mike probably didn't know that Dude was leaving."

"Wait, even though we're in Tech Team, we're being stupid!" Caleb burst out. "Teachers and pupils don't have keys to the headteacher's office. That means I'm off the suspect list!" He grabbed Zoe's pen and drew five lines through his name.

A relieved smile broke across Zoe's face as Caleb handed the pen back. It would have been horrible if Caleb really was the perpetrator.

"Sonja's off the list too!" Zoe crossed out Sonja's name.

"So is our top suspect," Jaden said. "You have to take Ms Kinney off the list – Madison and Mike too."

"There's only one suspect left," Zoe announced. "Mr Figgis. He has keys to everywhere in the school."

"There's still Dude too. Although I'm not sure why it would've smashed up its own leg," Caleb admitted.

"You can't think of a reason because there isn't one," Zoe insisted.

"You don't know that," Caleb said. "You keep expecting it to think like a human, but Dude is a robot. Who knows what motives it might have."

"You act like robots are–" Zoe began.

Jaden didn't let her finish. "Let's focus. We said we'd leave Dude off the list unless we got proof that he could ignore the sleep command. So Mr Figgis is our new top suspect. Agreed?"

Zoe and Caleb nodded, but neither looked happy.

"Before our Tech Team meeting after school, let's talk to Mr Figgis," Jaden said. "Maybe we'll find the evidence we need to close this case."

* * *

A soft melody caught Jaden's attention as he, Zoe and Caleb searched the halls for Mr Figgis that afternoon. This way!" he cried. "I hear 'Hey Jude'!"

"What?" Caleb asked as he followed Jaden.

"Mr Figgis told us he sings 'Hey Jude' whenever he gets scared," Zoe explained. "You were out getting signatures for your petition when we talked to him."

"'Hey Jude'? Weird," Caleb muttered.

Jaden led the way around the corner. Mr Figgis was cleaning the glass trophy case.

"Did you see another spider?" Zoe asked as she and the boys approached him.

Mr Figgis turned towards them. "No. But I had a bad scare last night. I'm not quite over it." His words came out quickly, and his voice was high. "I was cleaning in the headteacher's office, and that creepy robot was in there." The little hairs on the back of Jaden's neck prickled. Mr Figgis had just admitted he was at the scene of the crime.

"When I was vacuuming..." Mr Figgis let his words trail off.

"What? What happened?" Caleb demanded.

"I ... I swear it moved," Mr Figgis told them, his voice getting so high it squeaked. "I had to plug the vacuum into a different socket so that I could reach behind the receptionist's desk – and when I looked back up, that robot was in a different spot." He started humming again.

"I believe you!" Caleb told him.

Mr Figgis began to hum louder, then broke into song.

Jaden shook his head. Clearly, the caretaker was too upset to say anything more. "See you later, Mr Figgis."

As soon as Zoe, Caleb and Jaden were out of Mr Figgis's sight, they all started talking at once.

"He definitely had the chance to commit the crime. He was in the office during the time Dude was attacked," Jaden said.

"Mr Figgis is terrified of Dude. Maybe he grabbed that owl and smashed Dude's leg because he thought Dude was coming after him," Zoe said at the same time.

"Did you hear him say Dude was moving around when he should've been powered off? I knew he could ignore the command!" Caleb exclaimed, sounding almost as upset as Mr Figgis had.

Jaden held up one hand to get the other two to stop talking. "We need evidence. I say we search the supply room." Mr Figgis had a desk there, and it's where he went on his breaks.

Zoe nodded. "Let's go, while we know he's not in there."

Caleb walked quickly towards the supply room with Jaden and Zoe following him down the corridor. "Unlocked," Caleb said when he tried the door. They slipped inside, and Jaden shut the door behind him.

Zoe looked at the messy desk and shelves crammed with cleaning stuff. "Okay," she said. "We need to find something that connects Mr Figgis to the crime."

"He has screwdrivers." Caleb picked one up from the nearest shelf. "He would have needed a screwdriver to take Dude's panels off to drain the hydraulic fluid."

"Yeah, but lots of people have screwdrivers," Jaden said. "Keep looking."

Zoe opened one of the side drawers of the desk. "There's a car repair manual in here." She flipped to the index. "There's a section on hydraulic brakes. So Mr Figgis could know about hydraulics."

"A lot of people have car repair manuals. It doesn't prove anything," Caleb said.

"Wait a second – Mr Figgis would've had to touch Dude to drain the hydraulic fluid and to break his finger," Jaden said as he opened a cardboard box. "Do you think he could've done that? Or would he have been too scared?"

Zoe looked over at Caleb. "Would *you* touch Dude?" she asked.

"If I was close enough to touch him, he'd be close enough to touch me," Caleb replied. "So, no."

Jaden let out a frustrated sigh. He wondered how Sherlock Holmes would solve this case.

Zoe reached for the handle of the next drawer, then froze as the door to the supply room opened with a bang.

A loud voice demanded, "What do you think you're doing in here?"

14

Jaden felt like he had a super computer in his brain, because he came up with the perfect excuse instantly. An excuse that would get them out of trouble *and* tell them whether Mr Figgis was too afraid of Dude to touch him.

"Mrs Ram sent us to find you," Jaden said. "She wanted help moving the robot back to her room."

The anger seemed to drain from Mr Figgis as soon as Jaden mentioned the robot. He began to hum "Hey Jude".

"So could you help with the robot?" Jaden asked again.

Mr Figgis started nodding rapidly. "I could do that. Of course I could do that. It's my job to help out with things like that." As he stepped back into the corridor, his humming turned to soft singing.

"He's starting to sweat," Zoe whispered to Jaden and Caleb as they followed the caretaker down the corridor.

The closer Mr Figgis got to the headteacher's office, the louder he sang. When they turned the corner and the headteacher's open office door came into view, he sang so loud it was more like screaming than singing.

Mr Figgis is in The Zone, Jaden thought. *Should we tell him he doesn't really have to help with the robot?*

Before Jaden could decide, Mr Figgis jerked to a stop. "I can't do it! I can't touch it!" he shrieked. He sped off down the corridor in the opposite direction.

"I don't think he sabotaged Dude," Caleb said.

"Me neither," Zoe agreed. "He's far too scared of Dude to have touched him."

"Which means we have no suspects left," Jaden observed. "So who *did* hurt Dude?"

* * *

"Dr Wiley is going to pick up *our friend* tonight," Mrs Ram told the Tech Team later that day at their after-school meeting. She'd told them not to use Dude's name. She thought it would be better for him to stay powered down until he could be repaired. He was covered with a tarpaulin, standing next to Mrs Ram's usual table.

Just then, SpotBot walked past, whining. Zoe was too distracted to pet it. "We have to tell Mr Figgis that *our friend* won't be at school anymore," she said. "It'll make him feel so much better."

Caleb couldn't stop staring at Dude. "I don't like this," he whispered to Jaden and Zoe. "I'd rather see its face. If I could see its face, maybe I could work out what it's thinking."

"He's not thinking anything," Jaden told him. "He's powered off."

"Maybe," Caleb said. "Maybe not." He kept his eyes on the tarpaulin-covered robot and started humming "Hey Jude". If it helped Mr Figgis, maybe it would help him.

Zoe jumped up. "I'll go and ask Mrs Ram to take off the tarpaulin." As she walked towards the teacher, Caleb's voice rose until he was singing "Hey Jude" at full volume.

Suddenly he stopped singing and started screaming.

"It moved!" Caleb cried. "It can turn itself on! It can think for itself! It's going to take over the world!"

Benjamin let out a high moan. Antonio leaped to his feet. Abby scrambled to the top of her worktable. Sonja balled her hands into fists, ready for a fight.

Dude began to shuffle forward. Purple light glowed from beneath the tarpaulin.

Zoe hurried back over to Caleb. She grabbed his arm with both hands to keep him from running off. Jaden looked around the room, trying to decide who he should try to calm down first.

Meanwhile, SpotBot wandered across the carpet, completely ignoring the chaos in the room. It almost walked into a table leg, then turned in another direction, just as it had been programmed to do.

Mrs Ram darted after the robot and whipped off the tarpaulin. "Go to sleep, Dude," she said loudly.

Instantly, Dude went still.

"Everybody, please sit down," Mrs Ram called. When they'd all returned to their chairs, she said, "Now everybody take a deep breath."

"What happened?" Sonja demanded.

"I'm not sure," replied Mrs Ram, looking at Dude. "I powered him down as soon as I brought him here."

"He can ignore the command!" Caleb yelled. Then he started to hum again, although "Hey Jude" hadn't helped.

A light bulb suddenly went off in Jaden's head. "I have an idea!" he called out. He stood up and moved closer to the robot. "Hey, Jude," he said.

Dude's eyes rolled from side to side. His ear paddles came forward. "Hi, Jaden."

Jaden smiled. "Jude, go to sleep," he said. Dude went still.

Mrs Ram laughed. "I'll have to tell Dr Wiley that his robot's sound sensors need an upgrade. He can't tell the difference between 'Jude' and 'Dude'."

Dude looked around the room as soon as Mrs Ram said his name. "Everyone is looking at me," he said.

"I think you should rest for a while," Mrs Ram told him. "Go to sleep, Dude." The robot closed his eyes again.

Zoe smiled at Caleb. "See, he's not going to take over the world," she said. "There was a logical explanation. You just woke him up by singing Mr Figgis's song." Her eyes widened. "Mr Figgis's song! I bet he sang it every time he was near the robot. That means *our friend* was powered on part of every night after Mr Figgis came in to clean! The robot would've turned off after an hour. That's why he was always powered down in the morning."

"Merciful Minerva," Mrs Ram breathed, using one of Wonder Woman's favourite phrases.

"Then I was right!" Caleb exclaimed, jumping up. "The droid's the perpetrator. It smashed up our makerspace.

It made those spots of oil around the school and ruined your jumper."

Jaden frowned. "I still don't see any motive."

"You've never heard the term bad robot?" Caleb challenged. "It enjoys being evil."

"Even if he is evil, which he's not, why would he smash up his own leg? Even you said that didn't make sense, Caleb," Zoe protested. SpotBot whined again. It was right by her feet, so she bent down and patted it.

"I said it didn't make sense to a *human*!" Caleb replied.

Jaden stared at SpotBot. The solution to the mystery had just hit him with the force of Thor's hammer. "Look!" he cried. He quickly brought up a video of a dog chewing its own leg on his computer monitor. "The dog is being destructive because it's anxious. It's been left alone for too long."

Sonja planted her hands on her hips. "So? What's that got to do with anything?"

"That's why we programmed SpotBot to tear up its pillow if it didn't get petted for a long time," Zoe said. She wasn't sure why Jaden was showing the video, either.

"Nobody programmed *it* to break stuff or hurt itself," Caleb pointed out.

"He learns by observing," Jaden reminded everyone. "That's why he's here. To observe us and learn. But what if part of what he learned was how dogs behave?"

"That makes–" Benjamin began.

Without hesitation, Samuel finished his brother's sentence. "–logical sense." The twins grinned at each other. The Things were back!

"Right!" Zoe cried. Now she got it! *"Our friend* watched all those dog-behaviour videos with us. He saw dogs chewing up shoes and tearing up couches, and he heard a trainer explain that it's because they'd been alone too much." She gave a little hop as she made another realization. "We watched a clip about wolves using urine to mark their territory. I bet that's what *our friend* was doing by making those little pools of hydraulic fluid around the school. He was saying the school was his place."

"But how'd he leave the media centre?" Dylan asked.

"He went through Mr Leavey's office," Jaden explained. "Those doors aren't locked from the outside as the main ones are."

Caleb looked at the monitor as he thought about everything that had happened since Dude arrived. "And it was with us when we watched the clip of the dog chewing on its leg when it was anxious," he added. "I guess Dude really didn't like to be alone all night."

When Caleb said his name, Dude turned on and looked at him. "Do you think you will ever like me, Caleb?"

Caleb hesitated for a second. "I suppose," he answered slowly. How could he say no when all the robot had been trying to do was tell them he was lonely?

Zoe elbowed him in the ribs – hard.

"I mean, I like you already, Dude," Caleb said.

* * *

"Hey, Dude!" Jaden sang out when the robot passed him, Zoe and Caleb in the hall three weeks later.

Dude waved. "Hello, Zoe! Hello, Caleb! Hello, Jaden!"

"Your voice sounds brilliant," Zoe told him. She smiled at Mike and Megan, who were standing on either side of Dude. "Hanging out with the drama kids is good for you."

"That and the lessons we're all taking from Professor Brock," Mike answered.

Dr Wiley had been fascinated when he'd found out that Dude had learned dog behaviour while he was in the makerspace. He'd decided that he wanted Dude to spend even more time out in the real world.

Mrs Ram had been the one to suggest Dude join the drama club. She'd thought it might help him learn to put more emotion in his voice, so he could sound more human. Dr Wiley loved the idea and had even arranged for a drama professor from the university to give the drama pupils – including Dude! – some lessons.

"We're actually on our way to a lesson right now," Madison said. "Dude and I are going to do a scene together."

"See you later," Dude told Zoe, Jaden and Caleb. The robot gave a loud whistle. A few seconds later, SpotBot trotted around the corner. Tech Team had loaned Dude the robot dog for the time he was at their school. They both stayed powered on at night and kept each other company.

"Want to hear a joke?" Jaden asked. He could remember a centillion of them – that was a one followed by 303 zeros – now that everyone in Tech Team was getting along again, especially Caleb and Zoe.

Caleb nodded. "As long as it's not about a droid of doom."

About the author

Melinda Metz is the author of more than sixty books for teenagers and children, including *Echoes* and the young adult series Roswell High, the basis of the TV series *Roswell*. Her mystery book *Wright and Wong: Case of the Nana-Napper* (co-authored by the fabulous Laura J. Burns) was a juvenile Edgar finalist. Melinda lives in North Carolina, USA, with her dog, Scully, a pen-eater just like the dog who came before her.

About the illustrator

Heath McKenzie is a best-selling author and illustrator from Melbourne, Australia. Over the course of his career, he has illustrated numerous books, magazines, newspapers and even live television. As a child, Heath was often inventing things, although his inventions didn't always work out as planned. His inventions still only work some of the time ... but that's the fun of experimenting!

Glossary

artificial intelligence ability of a machine to think like a person; abbreviated "AI"

droid short for android; a robot that looks, thinks and acts in a very similar way to a human being

hydraulics system of pumps powered by fluid forced through pipes or chambers

interact talk or do things with other people, groups or things

motive reason why a person did something

perpetrator someone who has committed a crime

petition document that many people sign to show they want a person or organization to change something

program series of instructions written in a computer language

sabotage deliberately damage or destroy something so that it no longer works correctly

suspect person who might have done something wrong and is being investigated

synthetic something that is manufactured or artificial rather than found in nature

tarpaulin large sheet of waterproof material, such as plastic or canvas, usually used to protect something from rain

Discussion questions

1. People don't always use their words to tell others how they're feeling. Sometimes they use body language. Talk about the ways people show different emotions through their actions.

2. When you were reading, who did you think committed the crimes? Discuss why you suspected that character, using examples from the story.

3. Dude was built to tutor children. Imagine you are designing your own robot. Talk about what it would do and how it would help humans.

Writing prompts

1. The Tech Team members all had different opinions about Dude, robots and artificial intelligence. Make two lists: one about how a robot that thinks for itself can be good and one about how it might be bad.

2. Write two paragraphs about a time when you disagreed with your friend. How did you work out your disagreement?

3. Attending drama lessons helped Dude to improve his voice. Think about other subjects that would help Dude. Write a new chapter where you take Dude to learn a new subject. What does Dude learn while he's with you?

Artificial intelligence

Artificial intelligence (AI) is the ability of computers and robots to carry out tasks and behaviours usually seen in intelligent beings. Intelligent beings (like humans) are able to learn from past experiences, reason, see and understand their environment, and problem solve. Developing artificial intelligence is a very complex process because most machines can only do exactly what they're programmed to do. Since the 1950s, researchers have been searching for ways to make our technology smarter and more independent.

A major goal in AI research is to make a machine that can think like a human. This is a special type of AI called strong AI. But you don't have to worry about droids of doom taking over the world anytime soon – researchers still have a lot of work to do before they create strong AI. Part of the problem is that scientists don't fully understand how humans think, learn and feel. It's hard to create an artificial brain if you don't first know how a human brain works.

Engineers have already created some very impressive AIs, though. Large computing systems can help doctors diagnose a patient by sorting through enormous amounts of information and deciding which disease is most likely. Technology companies are working on computer systems that allow a car to drive itself. There are even social robots like Dude. A robot called NAO is not only used to teach children about programming, but it's also being used to help teach children with autism, a developmental disorder that affects a person's ability to interact with others. As technology advances, we can only imagine the new and helpful ways artificial intelligence will be used next.

More adventure and science mysteries!

www.raintree.co.uk